SADDLEBACK *Classics*

A TALE OF TWO CITIES

CHARLES DICKENS

ADAPTED BY

Janet Lorimer

SADDLEBACK PUBLISHING, INC.

SADDLEBACK Classics

The Call of the Wild
A Christmas Carol
Frankenstein
The Adventures of Huckleberry Finn
The Red Badge of Courage
The Scarlet Letter
A Tale of Two Cities
Treasure Island

Development and Production: Laurel Associates, Inc.
Cover and Interior Art: Black Eagle Productions

SADDLEBACK PUBLISHING, INC.
3505 Cadillac Ave., Building F-9
Costa Mesa, CA 92626-1443

ISBN 1-56254-277-X

Printed in the United States of America
05 04 03   9 8 7 6 5 4 3 2 1

CONTENTS

A Season of Change

It was the best of times. It was the worst of times. It was the age of wisdom. It was the age of foolishness. It was the season of light. It was the season of darkness. It was the spring of hope. It was the winter of despair.

It was the year 1775.

The kings of England and France were neither very good nor very wise rulers. In France, the King and Queen, the Lords and Ladies of the court, and most of the rich people lived in great comfort. They behaved as if each day was a grand party. Although the common people did all the work, they were often hungry and wore only rags. In those days, many workers starved to death or died of illness or neglect. But their deaths did not touch the cold hearts of the rich.

* * * *

One cold winter's day, a man stepped off the coach at the seacoast town of Dover in England. He was a middle-aged man, dressed like a man of business. He went straight to the inn.

"My name is Mr. Lorry," the man said to the innkeeper. "I am from Tellson's Bank in London. I will need a room for myself and another room for a young lady. Miss Lucie Manette will arrive later today."

The innkeeper bowed. "Very good, sir."

After he had something to eat, Mr. Lorry left the inn and went for a walk on the beach. Although the day was cold and dreary, he walked for hours. Often, he paused to look out across the sea toward France. He seemed to have a lot on his mind.

Lucie Manette arrived a few hours later. The innkeeper showed her to Mr. Lorry's sitting room. As they greeted each other, Mr. Lorry studied her. "She has grown into a beautiful young woman," he thought. "Indeed, she looks a lot like her mother, with those blond curls and blue eyes."

When they were both seated, Lucie said,

"The bank sent me a letter saying there was surprising news of my long-dead father. Can you tell me what that means, Mr. Lorry?"

"It's hard to know just where to begin," Mr. Lorry said with a troubled sigh. "Twenty years ago, I did some work for a famous French doctor named Dr. Manette."

Lucie gasped. "That was my *father*!"

"Dr. Manette had married an English woman," Mr. Lorry went on.

"My father died when I was very small," Lucie said. "My dear mother lived only two years after that. When she died, I was left an orphan." Lucie paused and looked closely at Mr. Lorry. "Were *you* the man who brought me to England?" she asked.

Mr. Lorry nodded. "Yes, but now I must ask you a question. What if your father had *not* died? What if he had been put in prison by someone who hated him? What if your mother begged the King for news about your father—but no one would help her?"

Lucie's face turned pale. She fell on her knees and grasped Mr. Lorry's hand. "Please tell me the truth!" she exclaimed.

"Your father is alive," Mr. Lorry said.

Lucie stared at him. "*No*, that cannot be! It must be his ghost!" she cried.

Mr. Lorry shook his head. "Your father is greatly changed, but he is not a ghost. He is not in good health, but he is alive. He has been released from prison. Now he is staying in the house of a former servant, a man named Monsieur Defarge. Tomorrow, we will go to Paris to rescue your father. Then we will bring him home to England."

Late the next day, Mr. Lorry and Lucie arrived in Paris. Their carriage drove down a narrow, dirty street. It stopped in front of a wine shop owned by Monsieur and Madame Defarge. Lucie saw many poor, ragged people huddled outside the door. Some were so thin and pale they looked like skeletons. Lucie shivered.

Just as she and Mr. Lorry went into the wine shop, a delivery cart came down the street. Suddenly one of the wooden barrels of wine rolled off the cart. It broke when it hit the rough cobblestones of the street. The red wine splashed like blood across the stones. At once the crowd of poor people ran into the street and fell on their knees to drink the wine. They scooped up the wine in their hands. They wet handkerchiefs in the puddles of wine and sucked the cloth. They squeezed the dirty wine into the mouths of their thin, ragged children.

The red wine stained the street and the hands and faces of the people. One man rose from his knees. He dipped his fingers into the red mud of the street. On the wall behind him, he wrote the word *Blood*.

Almost at once, another man took a handkerchief and wiped the word from the wall. "Not *now*!" he whispered. "Soon the streets will run with blood—not wine. But the time is not yet right. Be patient."

Inside the wine shop, wooden tables and benches stood about the room. Behind the counter a middle-aged woman sat, knitting.

"Madame Defarge?" Mr. Lorry asked.

The woman looked up. Seeing that the strangers were very well-dressed, a cold, unfriendly look came into her eyes. "I am Madame Defarge," she said.

"Good day, madame. May I speak with your husband?" said Mr. Lorry.

Monsieur Defarge came forward to greet them with a smile. Lucie saw that he was the man who had erased the word *Blood* from the stone wall. "How may I help you?" Defarge asked with a smile.

"We are here to see Dr. Manette," said Mr. Lorry.

Defarge's smile vanished. "Come with me," he said in a gruff voice.

He led them up a dark, narrow staircase. Lucie saw garbage scattered about on the landing. The cold, damp air smelled sour. Trembling, Lucie drew her warm cloak tighter around her.

At the top of the stairs, Defarge took out a key and unlocked the door to an attic room.

"Why is he locked up?" Lucie asked. "Hasn't he been locked up long enough?"

"He was locked up for 18 years," Defarge answered. "If we left the door open, he would not understand. He would be afraid."

"How can that be?" asked Mr. Lorry. "How can a man be so fearful?"

Defarge turned to them. His eyes flashed with anger. "*How?* Oh, let me tell you, sir. It is *fear* that butters the stale crusts we eat. It is fear that we wear like a rough shirt. Fear is the only friend who walks with us day and night. There is good reason for so much fear. Here in France terrible things are done to the people every day."

Defarge pushed the door open. Inside, the attic room was dark and narrow with a low ceiling. A small window let gray light into the room. Next to the window, an old man was sitting on a low bench. He was thin and pale and dressed in rags. His gray hair and beard were long and tangled.

When the visitors walked into the room, the old man did not look up. They saw that he was busy making a pair of shoes.

"You have a visitor," Defarge said to Dr. Manette.

"Dr. Manette, do you know who I am?" Mr. Lorry asked, stepping into the dim light. "Do you remember me?"

The old man gazed at Mr. Lorry. For a moment, it almost seemed as if he did

remember. But then he frowned and shook his head. With a sigh, he returned to work.

"Well?" Defarge asked Mr. Lorry. "Do you know him?"

Mr. Lorry nodded. "Oh, yes, but he has changed so much. And yet, for one moment, I saw the face I remember from so long ago."

"Why is he making a pair of shoes?" Lucie asked. "My father was a doctor."

"He learned to make shoes in prison," Defarge said. "Now that is all he knows. He does not even remember his real name. He calls himself by his cell number." Defarge turned to Dr. Manette. "Can you tell us your name, sir?"

Dr. Manette looked sadly at Defarge and said, "105, North Tower."

Lucie stepped closer to Dr. Manette. He peered at her. "Who are you?" he asked.

Lucie's eyes filled with tears. She sat down next to him on the bench. "My name is not important right now," she said softly. "For now it is enough for you to know that you are safe."

Dr. Manette gazed at her blond hair. "That *voice!*" he exclaimed. With shaking fingers he reached out and touched her hair. "Your golden curls. They're the same as—" He shook his head. "What is your name, my gentle angel?"

Lucie put her arms around the man's thin shoulders. "I will tell you my name later," she said. "For now, believe me that your pain is over. I have come to take you home to England."

2 Darnay on Trial

Five years went by. It was now 1780. France and England had fought against each other in many wars. The countries were like two people who are polite in public, but then say rude things about each other in private.

In London, Lucie and Dr. Manette lived quietly in a pleasant house. Dr. Manette had regained his health and his memory. He now remembered his life before he went to prison. He was able to practice medicine again.

Dr. Manette remembered a lot about the 18 years he'd spent in prison. But he did not remember *everything*. Sometimes this upset him.

In the same year, 1780, a handsome young Frenchman named Charles Darnay was going on trial in London. Darnay lived in England, but often traveled to France. He had been accused of giving English secrets to the French King.

On the day the trial began, many English people crowded into the courtroom. They hoped Darnay would be found guilty. They wanted to see his head cut off.

Two people in the courtroom did not feel that way. Lucie Manette and her father had been called to testify against Darnay. They had met him on the boat that returned them home to England.

The lawyer for the court called Lucie to the stand. "Miss Manette, have you seen the prisoner before?"

Lucie glanced over at the handsome Frenchman. Charles Darnay drew in his breath sharply. Lucie was so *beautiful*!

Lucie nodded. She told the court how she and her father had met the man. "My father was not very well at the time. Mr. Darnay was very kind to us."

"And what did you and Mr. Darnay talk about?" asked the lawyer for the court.

"We talked about the Revolutionary War in America," said Lucie. "Mr. Darnay said that George Washington might become more famous than our English King George." At that, people in the crowd gasped, and even the judge frowned. "Of course, it was all said in fun," Lucie added quickly. "I hope that what I've said won't hurt Mr. Darnay."

The lawyer for the court called other people to speak against the accused. One man had worked for Darnay. "My master made a lot of visits to France." The servant's lips curled into a mean smile. "I saw important-looking papers on his desk. Sometimes he had them in his pockets before he left for a trip. In fact, I even saw him show these papers to Frenchmen."

The people in the courtroom roared with anger. They had already made up their minds that Darnay was guilty.

But the trial wasn't over yet. Darnay's lawyer also had questions for the servant. "Did you not have reason to be angry at Mr. Darnay?" the lawyer asked. "Didn't he fire you for stealing a silver coffee pot?"

"No," the servant said quickly. "It wasn't a coffee pot. It was just a little pitcher—

and it wasn't even made of silver."

Darnay's lawyer smiled. The people in the courtroom burst out laughing. The lawyer for the court frowned. He knew that no one would believe the witness now.

Another witness was certain he had seen Darnay getting secrets from soldiers near a military post. The jury seemed to believe this witness. Lucie felt her hopes sink.

"Are you sure it was Charles Darnay you saw?" asked Darnay's lawyer.

The witness nodded. "Yes, I am sure."

"Look at my helper," said the lawyer, pointing to a man sitting next to him. "He is Mr. Sydney Carton." The man stood up and took off his wig. "Now look again at the prisoner," said the lawyer.

The witness looked from Carton to Darnay and back again. "Oh, my! They look a lot alike," said the witness.

"And are you still sure that it was the *prisoner* you saw at the military post?"

The witness shook his head. "No . . . I can't be sure," he said.

The jury found Darnay innocent. After

he was freed, the Manettes congratulated Darnay on his escape from death.

Charles Darnay gazed at Lucie. Then he took her hand and kissed it. "Thank you," he said, "for helping me."

No one seemed to notice the look on Dr. Manette's face. It was as if he were trying to remember something—something painful from long ago.

"Come, Father," Lucie said. "It's time to go home now."

Sydney Carton had been standing to one side, watching Darnay and the Manettes.

When the Manettes left in their carriage, he stepped forward. "You must be hungry after all this," Carton said to Darnay. "Will you join me for dinner? I know a good place to eat, a little tavern near here."

Darnay smiled and nodded. "I owe you thanks for your help today," he said, as they walked to the tavern.

Before long the men were sitting at a table, enjoying a good meal. Although they looked very much alike, the two men were quite different. Carton's clothes were wrinkled and stained. He looked as if he didn't care much about himself—and he drank far too much wine. On the other hand, Darnay's clothes were clean and neat. And he sat up tall and straight, while Carton slumped in his chair.

As they ate, Carton studied Darnay. When he had finished his meal, Darnay leaned back in his chair. "I am so happy!" he exclaimed. "I can hardly believe that I am free. It feels so good to be a living part of this world again."

A dark look crossed Carton's face. He shoved his plate aside, reaching for his wine glass. "I would like to *forget* that I am alive and in this world! I care for no one, and no one cares for me. I have nothing to be happy about. Except, of course, the wine!" Grinning, he raised his glass, but there was no happiness in his smile.

Darnay gazed at Carton. "I am sorry for you," he said. "There's a lot more to life than wine."

Carton's lips curled in a sneer. "Don't be so sure. You may be happy now—but you don't know what tomorrow will bring."

Darnay stood up. "No, but I am too happy to let you upset me. I will say goodnight now. Maybe we will meet again."

After Darnay left the tavern, Carton picked up a candle. He walked to a mirror on the tavern wall and gazed at himself in the candle's glow. "Ah, Carton, look at yourself! Look at what you have become," he said to himself. "There was a time when you were very much like Darnay. You walked tall and took pride in the way you spoke and the way you looked. Now look at you!" Carton sighed bitterly. "Why don't you be honest? You *envy* Darnay because the beautiful Lucie is in love with him. You saw the way she looks at him."

Then Sydney Carton stumbled back to his table. He rested his head on his arms. "If things were different, Lucie might be in love with *you*," he moaned. "Then you would be happy because you love her, too." As the candle burned low, he fell asleep.

# 3 Death to the Marquis!

In Paris, the Marquis St. Evremonde was on his way home from a party. Sitting against the plush cushions of his handsome carriage, he was pleased that his carriage was going so fast. He liked hearing the poor people cry out in surprise and fear as it raced down the narrow street. The lives of the poor workers meant nothing to the Marquis.

Suddenly the carriage rocked and the horses reared. The Marquis heard a terrible cry. They had hit something! The driver pulled on the reins to stop the horses. Leaning out the carriage door, the Marquis saw a poor man picking up the body of a child from the street. The man was sobbing.

"Driver," the Marquis called out in a cross voice, "what is wrong with that man? Why is he crying?"

"A child was run over by the carriage," said the driver. "The child was his son."

The poor man raised his head and glared at the Marquis. His tears were mixed with a look of rage. "You *killed* him!" he cried.

Another man stepped out of the crowd to comfort the father. The Marquis did not know that it was Defarge, the owner of the wine shop.

The Marquis frowned. "What's wrong with you people? Can't you take care of your own children?" he cried out. "That nasty little beast might have hurt my beautiful horses." Reaching in his pocket, the Marquis pulled out a gold coin and tossed it at the father of the dead boy. "Take this and stop crying. It annoys me. Driver, let's go!"

Defarge caught the coin. As the carriage started to move forward, he tossed it back through the window. The Marquis quickly leaned forward.

"*Stop!*" the Marquis ordered. "Driver, hold the horses. Who threw the coin back at me?" He glared at the people in the crowd. He did not notice the looks of hatred on their faces. "You stupid beasts!" he exclaimed. "I would be happy to ride over *all* of you and wipe you from the earth!"

From the wine shop, Madame Defarge had seen everything. As the carriage drove away, Madame Defarge took up her knitting. The knitting needles clicked peacefully, but there was murder in her eyes.

When the Marquis reached his mansion, he found his nephew waiting for him. In France, the nephew's last name was St. Evremonde. In England, he went by the name of Charles Darnay.

"So, you are here at last," the Marquis said to Darnay. "It took you long enough to come home."

"I came back only because I had to," Darnay said. "Don't you understand, Uncle, that times are changing and that *we* must change, too? Our family hurts everyone who comes between us and the things we want. Our name is the most hated name in France."

The Marquis shrugged. "So what? Why do you care if the workers hate us? They are nothing—they are *nobody*! They are like ungrateful dogs that must be trained."

Darnay glared at his uncle. "I *hate* the kind of life you live! I would be ashamed to treat people the way you do. And I tell you now—if I had your land and money, I would give it all up just as I have given up France."

The Marquis smiled a cruel smile. "Just remember that this is not your property—not yet." He stood and stretched. "I am going to bed now, Charles."

The Marquis went upstairs. Like every room in the house, his bedroom was very grand. The curtains were made of the finest velvet. The carpet was soft and thick. There were many servants to help him.

As he climbed into bed, the Marquis did not think once about the child who had died under his horses' hooves. The father's terrible sadness had been forgotten.

The next morning, the Marquis did not come down for breakfast. When the servants went to wake him, they found him dead in his bed! He had been stabbed through the heart. A note next to his cold, dead body read: *"Death to the Marquis!"*

No one knew who had killed the Marquis. The St. Evremonde family had many enemies, so it might have been anyone. Most people thought the child's father must have done it, but they did not say so out loud.

Charles Darnay went back to England.

A year went by. It was now 1781. While working as a teacher, Darnay often visited Dr. Manette and Lucie. Their peaceful home was like a safe harbor for Darnay. A housekeeper named Miss Pross took care of the family. She had cared for Lucie ever since Lucie's mother had died. Now the faithful servant cared for Lucie and her father.

Mr. Lorry and Sydney Carton also visited the Manettes. These visits were always pleasant times, even for Sydney Carton. Lucie was always kind to him. Her friendship was important to Carton.

One day, when he knew the doctor was alone, Charles Darnay went to see Dr. Manette. "I must talk to you, sir," Darnay said, "about something very important. I love Lucie and I want to marry her."

Dr. Manette sighed. "Have you told Lucie how you feel?" the doctor asked. Darnay shook his head. "Then you must," the doctor said. "If Lucie feels the same way about you, I will allow you and Lucie to get married."

"Thank you, sir," Darnay said. "But first, there is something else I must tell you. There must not be any secrets between us. You already know that I am French. Now I want you to know my real name and why I now live in England."

"No!" the doctor exclaimed. Suddenly he seemed very upset. "Do not say another word, Charles. If you and Lucie marry, I will listen to what you want to tell me on your wedding day. Tell me nothing until then."

4 The Defarges Plan Revenge

Charles Darnay was not the only man who loved Lucie Manette. Sydney Carton could not get Lucie out of his thoughts. One day when Carton was visiting the Manettes, he took Lucie aside. "Miss Manette," he said, "please look me in the eye. I want you to know that I am in love with you."

Lucie drew back in surprise. Sydney Carton did not look well. His face was pale, and his hands shook a little. There were dark shadows under his eyes.

He saw her look of amazement. "I do not expect you to love me in return," he said quickly. "I know that is not possible. I am not good enough for you. Too much wine has ruined me. I would never ask you to share my sad life."

Lucie's surprise turned to pity. "Oh,

27

Mr. Carton, I know you have a kind heart. No matter what you say, you are a good man. It's not too late to change. Let me help you! In time, you could become the kind of person you want to be."

Carton shook his head. "No—it's too late for that. I do not have the heart for it. But thank you for listening, Miss Manette. Please, think of me kindly."

"Why, of course I will, Mr. Carton," Lucie said earnestly. *"Always."*

"You must know there is nothing I wouldn't do for you," Carton exclaimed. "I would give my life for you if I had to!"

"Please, Mr. Carton, I hope it will never come to that," Lucie said, her eyes filling with tears.

"You are too kind to me," Carton said softly. He patted her hand. "I must go now. God bless you, Miss Manette."

It saddened Lucie that Carton would not try to help himself, but her sadness did not last. Lucie had many good things to think about. The most wonderful thing, of course, was her marriage to Charles Darnay.

When their wedding day finally arrived, Charles Darnay asked Dr. Manette if they could speak alone. The old man nodded. He led Darnay to a small, quiet room.

"Doctor Manette, the time has come," Darnay said. "I must tell you now what you would not let me tell you before. The name that I use—Darnay—was my mother's maiden name. I have used her name since I left France. I could not bear to use my father's and my uncle's name."

Dr. Manette said nothing. Darnay went on. "My real name is Evremonde," he said at last. "Since my father and my uncle are dead, I am now the Marquis St. Evremonde."

Dr. Manette's face went pale. "Did I hear you correctly? Did you say—" He paused, almost as if it hurt him to say the words. "Surely you didn't say your name is *St. Evremonde?*" the doctor gasped.

Darnay looked puzzled. "Yes, I did. Is something wrong?"

The doctor seemed to be having trouble breathing. "No, no," he exclaimed. "Go on!"

"I have given up my rights to the family

fortune," Darnay went on. "My property is being used to help the people. As you know, I am a teacher. I earn my living through my own hard work."

More color came into Dr. Manette's face, but he was still upset. He took Darnay by the arm. "Promise me one thing. Tell no one else your true name."

Darnay nodded. "I promise you, sir."

A few hours later, Lucie Manette and Charles Darnay were married.

Meanwhile, in Paris, an Englishman

walked into the wine shop. He was an old friend of Defarge's. The Englishman took a seat at one of the wooden tables. Defarge brought the man a glass of wine.

"Tell me," said the Englishman, "were you and your wife the people who took care of Dr. Manette when he left prison?"

Defarge nodded his head. "Why do you ask?" he said suspiciously.

"Did you happen to hear that the doctor's daughter has married a Frenchman?"

A strange look came into Defarge's eyes. "No," he said. "We did not hear about that."

"In England, the Frenchman goes by the name of Darnay—but he is *really* the Marquis St. Evremonde."

Defarge's mouth tightened into a grim line. "If that is true," he said, "I hope for his wife's sake that fate will keep him out of France. His family has brought nothing but trouble to our people."

When the man left, Madame Defarge smiled sourly. Her knitting needles clicked faster. "His luck will take him where he must go," she said to herself. "His luck will lead him to the end that is to end him."

Defarge turned to his wife. "Did you hear that? Did you hear what our friend said about Darnay—and who he really is?"

Madame Defarge's needles flew faster. Only Defarge knew that the stitches in her yarn were a kind of code. She was knitting a list of names. The nobles and other rich people whose names she was listing would not come to a good end.

Madame Defarge smiled. "Have no fear, husband. Darnay is listed. And now his new family is also listed—for death."

5

A Time of Terror

Time passed. Charles and Lucie lived happily with Dr. Manette in London. Within the year, Lucie gave birth to a little girl. They named her after her mother.

Sydney Carton and Mr. Lorry often came to visit. Sydney was as fond of little Lucie as if she were his own child. He would play with her by the hour and bounce her on his knee. He read stories to her at bedtime. Whenever he appeared, little Lucie greeted him with cries of joy.

On the night of July 14, 1789, Mr. Lorry came to visit. He looked very tired.

"I didn't think I would ever get out of the bank tonight," he said. "There is trouble in Paris. The rich people are sending us their money and jewelry for safekeeping."

"What? That doesn't sound good," said

Charles. He looked very worried. "I'm afraid the workers have finally had enough suffering. They hate the rich for treating them so badly. I cannot blame them."

Then a sudden roll of thunder made Lucie jump. She walked to the window and looked out at the cloudy night sky. "Oh, look, a big storm is coming," Lucie said. "I have felt uneasy all day."

"Yes," Charles said. "There *is* something strange in the air. It feels as if something terrible is about to happen."

Across the channel, in Paris, another kind of storm was about to break. It would start in the Defarges' wine shop. From all over the city, the poor workers were coming to the Defarges to get weapons. Soon the crowd spilled out into the street. Now they were not calling out for wine—but for blood!

Defarge jumped to the top of a table. "Are the people of France ready?" he roared, shaking his fist. The crowd roared back. Yes, the people were ready. They wanted blood.

"Let us lead as many men as we can," Defarge shouted. The crowd cheered. Over their heads they waved their guns and knives, their swords and axes.

Defarge turned to his wife. For once Madame Defarge had put her knitting aside. Now she was holding an axe. The sharp blade gleamed in the candlelight. "And what will *you* do, my dear?" Defarge asked.

She lifted the axe high over her head and shook it. Her eyes glowed with cruel fire. "I will lead the women," she cried. "We women can kill as easily as men can."

Defarge turned back to face the crowd. "Come!" he shouted. "We are ready! Let us march to the Bastille!"

The Bastille was a huge, stone prison. Over the years, many poor people had been locked up there. Most had been tortured. All had suffered, and many had died. The Bastille was a hated symbol of cruelty.

The crowd poured out of the wine shop. Snarling like hungry animals, the people marched toward the Bastille. In the city, alarm bells rang. Drums beat. As the crowd pushed closer to the Bastille, more and more people poured into the streets.

Before long, some 20,000 people were gathered outside the Bastille. They pushed at the huge gates. The prison guards fired into the crowd, but where one man dropped, two more took his place. The guards soon saw that they had no chance against so many angry people.

Then suddenly a white flag rose up on the roof. The guards had surrendered! The crowd cheered as the gates opened wide. In a mad rush the mob swept into the prison's courtyard. Defarge led the way.

"Open the cells! Set the prisoners free!" someone shouted.

Defarge grabbed a guard by the collar and put a knife to the man's throat. "Take us to Cell 105 in the North Tower," he ordered. Defarge shoved the guard ahead of him, and several other men followed.

When they reached Cell 105, Defarge made the guard open the door. Inside, he held up his torch and looked at the stone walls closely. "I am looking for the letters A.M.," he said to his men.

Defarge's men began to search. Then

suddenly, Defarge gave a shout. "Look—here they are!" he said. "A.M. These letters stand for Alexandre Manette—Doctor Manette. This was his cell."

"Why does it matter so much?" asked one of the men.

Defarge handed his torch to the man. Then he pulled a crowbar from his belt and began to loosen a stone from the wall. Holding the torch close, he peered into a small, dark hole. Then he reached in and pulled out a handful of papers. "Here is the evidence I came to find," he said. "These are important secret papers."

"What do they say?" asked the man.

Defarge shook his head. "Not now," he said. "Later I will show them to you. Right now we must join the others. Come with me. Our fight is not over!"

Defarge hurried back down the stairs. Soon he was caught up in the crowd again. He saw that the people had found the warden of the Bastille. With horrible shrieks, they beat and stabbed him until he fell dead.

Madame Defarge put her foot on the dead

man's neck. She raised the axe over her head and brought it down hard. Someone grabbed the man's head as it rolled from his body. It was put on the sharp end of a long pole. The pole was lifted high in the air so that everyone could see the terrible prize. The crowd cheered. Soon more poles with newly cut-off heads were raised.

These deaths did not satisfy the people's terrible hunger. They had been treated badly for so long that nothing, it seemed, could stop their desire for revenge. At last the poor workers were striking back.

A time of terror had begun. All across France, mobs of poor people rose up to kill the rich. One mob found a rich man hiding from them. The man had once told the workers that if they were hungry, they could eat grass. In fury the mob dragged him into the streets and beat him.

Someone threw a rope over a lamp post. They tied a noose at one end and put it around the man's neck. He screamed for mercy, but no one listened. After he was hanged, they cut off his head.

Many rich Frenchmen fled to England. Taking only what they could carry with them, they wondered if they would ever see their homes in France again.

Now it was the poor workers who ruled France. All across the country, they broke into the homes of the rich. They took food, clothing, and furniture. They burned the homes to the ground. The killing had become a madness. Even the decent, kindly rich were blamed for things they had not done. Before the bloodbath would end, many good and innocent people were doomed to die.

6 Darnay Goes to Prison

One foggy afternoon three years later, Charles Darnay sat in Mr. Lorry's office. The two men were talking. "I'm afraid I must leave for Paris soon," Mr. Lorry said.

Darnay looked worried. "Must you go now?" he asked. "Paris is not a safe place."

Mr. Lorry straightened some papers on his desk. "It's safe enough for the English, Charles. It's only the French who are in danger of having their heads cut off." He sighed. "I have important bank business. In fact, I must leave tonight."

As Darnay stood up to leave, Mr. Lorry added, "By the way, I have an important letter that was secretly brought to the bank from France. But I don't know the man it's addressed to. Would you by any chance know where I could find him?"

Darnay took the letter that Mr. Lorry handed him. He gasped when he read the name on the envelope. Mr. Lorry was busy putting his papers together. He did not see the fear on Darnay's face.

The letter was addressed to the Marquis St. Evremonde! Darnay remembered his promise not to tell anyone his real name. "I know the man very well," he said calmly. "I'll make sure he gets it. Goodbye, Mr. Lorry, and good luck to you on your trip."

As soon as Darnay was outside the bank, he opened the letter. It was from a former servant of his named Gabelle. The letter came from a prison in Paris.

"I have been arrested and put in prison. If you cannot help me, I shall lose my life. I am accused of working against France when I was managing your property. I explained that I did not collect any rent from the people who live on your land. I told them that you were good to your tenants, but they do not believe me. They do not listen. They want to know

41

where you are, and they think I can tell them. I hope this letter gets to you. I beg you to return to Paris to help gain my release. I have been true to you, sir. I pray you will be true to me."

When Darnay finished reading, he closed his eyes as if in pain. After his uncle had been murdered, the St. Evremonde mansion and land outside Paris had become Darnay's property. Darnay had put Gabelle in charge. He had told Gabelle to help the people who lived on the land. If the people had turned on Gabelle, it was a sign of the madness in France.

"Poor Gabelle!" Darnay exclaimed. "I should not have left him to manage by himself. My life in England has been happy. I have forgotten about my duties in France."

Stuffing the letter into his pocket, Darnay walked quickly down the street. "I must go to Paris at once," he said to himself. "I will send a letter to let Lucie know where I've gone. I'll send it after I leave, however. I know she will be very upset when she finds that I've returned to France."

Reaching France, Darnay found things were much worse than he had imagined. The workers were now in control of everything— and they were *still* hungry for blood! Every town gate was guarded by angry people. They questioned anyone who tried to pass through.

The workers who had risen up against the nobles now had a title. They were called *Citizens*. The Citizens wore rough red caps with a knot of red, white, and blue ribbon. The colors were important. To the Citizens, these colors stood for freedom. Yet now, strangely, almost no one *had* freedom!

Darnay was stopped by a guard. Looking closely, the man saw that Darnay wore fine clothes. "You say you are a Frenchman," the guard said. "Why have you risked the guillotine by coming back to France? Why did you leave in the first place? Where are you going now?"

"I am going to Paris," Darnay said. "I have business there."

"Indeed," said the guard, coldly. "Then I will send a guard to Paris with you."

"I can find my own way," Darnay said.

"I assure you that I don't need—"

"Be quiet!" the guard shouted. "You will do just as you are told." He took another long look at Darnay. "Why, you were a *noble*, weren't you?" The guard's voice rose higher. His face turned ugly. "You will go to Paris under guard, *pig*!"

Arriving in Paris, Darnay was taken to see an officer of the people. It was none other than Monsieur Defarge! Now, of course, he was called Citizen Defarge. He knew who Darnay really was.

"You are St. Evremonde," Defarge said. "*Coward!* You ran away from France so you would be safe."

"I did not run away," Darnay said, "and I have come back of my own free will."

"You have not told us what we want to know," said Defarge. "You will be held in prison until we decide what to do with you."

Darnay gasped. "In prison? Under what law?" he cried angrily.

Defarge glared at Darnay. "We have new laws since you were here."

"Don't I have the right to a trial?"

"You have no rights," snarled Defarge. "It was people like you who once buried people like us in prison!"

"But no one was sent to prison by me," Darnay insisted. "I never did anything like that!"

Defarge only shrugged, and Darnay was quickly taken away.

Mr. Lorry, who was working at the Paris office of Tellson's Bank, did not know that Darnay was in France. A few days later, however, his door burst open. Mr. Lorry looked up in great surprise. "Lucie! Little Lucie! Dr. Manette! And even Miss Pross! Why are all of you here?"

Lucie tried to catch her breath. In great fear, her little daughter clung to her. Mr. Lorry saw that they were all very upset. "Charles is here in Paris," Lucie said. "He came to help an old friend—but he was stopped and sent to prison!"

"To *prison*?" Mr. Lorry cried out.

"My dear friend, do not worry so," Dr. Manette said. "*I* was once a prisoner in the Bastille. Now any man who helped to free the prisoners from the Bastille will help me. I know I can get Charles out of prison. That is why we have come."

Mr. Lorry sighed. "I hope you are right, but you must do so quickly." He reached for Lucie's hand. "My dear, you and the child are not safe. For now, I will put you in a little room behind my office. Miss Pross can rest with you there. Later I will find a place for you to rent. I think you may be here for a long while. At the moment, let me speak alone with your father."

When Lucie left, Mr. Lorry said, "Dr. Manette! The mobs are murdering the rich prisoners. Let me tell you about it."

The old man listened as Mr. Lorry talked. The banker's words painted a terrible picture. Every day small wooden carts rolled through the streets. The carts were filled with prisoners on their way to the guillotine. This was a terrible machine that cut people's heads off with a single stroke of a sharp blade.

"There's no time to waste!" Mr. Lorry cried at last. "If you think you can save Charles, you must do so at once."

7 Carton Offers Help

Dr. Manette went at once to La Force, the prison where Charles was being held. It was a very busy place.

"Please," Dr. Manette said to one of the guards, "take me to the citizens who are putting prisoners on trial."

In a few minutes, Dr. Manette found himself standing before Defarge. "Do you remember me?" Dr. Manette asked.

"Yes, of course," Defarge said.

"I was once a prisoner in the Bastille," Dr. Manette said. Defarge nodded. Other people stopped talking and turned to listen to what Dr. Manette was saying. "My son-in-law is a prisoner here now," Dr. Manette said. "I came to beg you for his liberty."

"He may be your son-in-law—but he is also the Marquis St. Evremonde," Defarge said sternly. "That means he is an enemy of the people. We cannot set him free, Dr. Manette, but you may be assured that we will keep him safe. I promise."

"May I see him?" Dr. Manette asked.

Nodding, Defarge ordered a guard to show Dr. Manette to Darnay's cell. The guard led the way up a set of narrow stone stairs. Dr. Manette felt sick. The sight and smell of cold damp stone reminded him of his long, unhappy years in the Bastille.

At last the guard unlocked a heavy wooden door. Dr. Manette peered into the cell and then stepped inside. His heart sank as the heavy door slammed shut. On the floor was a straw mattress. Charles Darnay was slumped in a chair by a small table. When he saw his visitor, he jumped to his feet. "Dr. Manette!" he cried in disbelief. "What are you doing here?"

"I am here to stay with you, Charles. I want to be sure that no harm comes to you. I will do all I can to see that you are not turned over to that terrible mob outside."

Two days went by. Lucie was almost sick

with worry. Then, on the night of the second day, a note came to her from Charles. Dr. Manette had given the note to Defarge and his wife. They, in turn, took the note to Mr. Lorry. Mr. Lorry took the Defarges to Lucie.

"Dr. Manette asked me to bring this note to you. It is from your husband," Defarge said.

Lucie took the note and quickly read it.

"Be brave, my dear one. I am well. Your father makes sure I come to no harm. Give our daughter a kiss from me."

Lucie's smile was filled with joy. "Thank you, Monsieur Defarge. You have brought us comforting news. My husband is safe!"

Feeling someone tugging at her hand, Lucie looked down and saw her little daughter. The child was peeking at Defarge from behind her mother's skirts.

At that moment, Madame Defarge stepped forward. She had been studying Lucie with a cold look in her eye. Now she came closer to stare at the child.

"I came with my husband to get a good look at you. Now I have seen you both—

the wife and the child of the prisoner, St. Evremonde."

Little Lucie shrank back in fear. Her mother held the little girl close. They watched as the Defarges walked away.

Lucie shivered. "That woman!" she exclaimed to Mr. Lorry. "There is something dark and evil in her. Whenever I see her, it is as if a dark shadow is cast over me and everything I hope for."

A few days later, Dr. Manette came to visit Lucie. "The worst danger is over," he said with a sigh. "Charles is safe—at least for now."

"Will Charles ever be free to return to England?" Lucie asked.

Dr. Manette shook his head. "I don't know, my dear. We must wait and see."

More time passed. Dr. Manette, Lucie, and little Lucie stayed in Paris, waiting. Every day the guillotine took more lives. Thousands of people had now died. Both the King and Queen of France had lost their heads. The great Lords and Ladies had lost their heads as well. Now the prisons were filling up with all kinds of people—young girls and boys, old men and women, people born with money, and people born poor. It did not seem to matter.

Each day Lucie wondered if this would be her husband's last day of life. Each day the carts carried more prisoners to the guillotine. Its sharp blade was like the mouth of a hungry monster—and the prisoners' blood was the monster's red wine!

Sometimes Lucie would stand outside the prison and gaze up at the window of her husband's cell. Sometimes she took her child with her. Even though they could not see Darnay, she hoped *he* could see them. Every day she wondered if she would ever again see her beloved husband alive.

Then Lucie learned that her long wait was almost over. The very next day Charles was to be put on trial.

That same night there was a knock on Mr. Lorry's office door. Mr. Lorry was surprised to find Sydney Carton on his doorstep. "Hello. What are you doing here?" Mr. Lorry asked politely.

"Please, sir—I know that Charles Darnay is in prison," Carton said in a worried tone. "I've come to see if there is anything I can do to help." Mr. Lorry told him that Darnay would be put on trial the next day. "Then I shall wait and see what happens," Carton said.

8 Darnay Faces New Charges

The Paris courtroom was packed with people. Most of them were wearing red caps. The men openly carried knives and guns. So did some of the women. Many people in the crowd were eating and drinking, talking and laughing loudly. They acted as if the trial was nothing but a show.

As Charles Darnay was brought into the courtroom, he thought about the time he had been put on trial in England. Once again his life was at stake. He stared out at the sea of faces—but only two stood out. One was the face of a cold-eyed woman looking up from her knitting. The other was his father-in-law's, a face filled with compassion.

Five judges were seated at a high bench in the front of the courtroom. These five men would decide if Charles was to live or die.

"Charles Darnay," called out one of the judges. "You are accused of being one of the noblemen who ran away from France. We have new laws now. They are very clear. Any nobleman who tries to return to France must be executed!"

Darnay felt his heart pounding. This time he did not have a lawyer to speak for him. He would have to defend himself as best he could. "I did not run from France, sir," Darnay said politely. "I left long before the revolution. Besides, the new law was passed *after* I came back to France. It would be unjust to punish me for breaking a law that was made after I returned."

"You lived in England for many years, didn't you?" the judge asked.

Darnay nodded. "I did, sir. When I left France, I gave up my title of Marquis and all the land and the money that went with that title. I wanted to make my own way in the world—to support myself with my own hard work. I did not choose to live off the people of France as so many rich people did."

A low hum arose from the people in the

crowded courtroom. Darnay saw them nod to each other. It seemed that they were pleased with his answers.

"While you lived in England, did you marry?" asked the judge.

"Yes, I did," Darnay said. "My wife is a Frenchwoman."

"And who is she?" asked the judge.

"Her name is Lucie Manette. She is the only child of Dr. Alexandre Manette." Darnay pointed toward Lucie's father. "He is sitting here in the courtroom."

"Tell the court why you came back to France, Mr. Darnay," said the judge.

Darnay shrugged. "After I gave up my title and my lands, I had no way to make a living in France. I went to England." Darnay went on to say that he was now a teacher. Finally, he told the court about the letter from Gabelle. "I came back to France to try to help my old friend," Darnay said.

"Sir, please, may I speak?" A man sitting in the front row was standing up. The judge nodded. The man came forward and identified himself as Gabelle. He had been set free only a few days before. "What Mr. Darnay says is true," said Gabelle. "I begged him to come back to France to help me."

Dr. Manette was also questioned. The people in the courtroom liked Dr. Manette. They all knew that he had once been a prisoner in the Bastille. They knew he had been put there by one of the nobles. That made Dr. Manette seem like one of them.

"My son-in-law is truly a good and decent man," Dr. Manette said. "He was a great help to my daughter and me after I was set free from the Bastille. We became friends. For many years he has been very kind to us."

"Enough!" a judge called out. "I believe that we've heard all we need to hear. We are ready to vote."

Darnay held his breath as the votes were counted. Every vote called for Charles Darnay to be set free!

When the judge announced the verdict, the crowd went wild. Many smiling people rushed forward to wish Darnay well. They were happy for him.

Then suddenly, Darnay found himself lifted up by the red-capped Citizens. They carried him home on their shoulders! As Darnay rode home in victory, he didn't notice that two people were missing from the crowd. Defarge and his wife were not among those who wished him well.

Darnay was overjoyed to be back with his family. He hugged each of them in turn. "Lucie, my dearest wife, I am safe at last! If your good father had not spoken out, I might not be here with you now. He helped me as no one else in France could have done."

"Oh, dear Father, I cannot thank you enough!" Lucie exclaimed.

Dr. Manette smiled and patted her hand. "My sweet child, I am happy for us all."

This was indeed a special day. After being apart for so long, the family was finally together again. They sat together after dinner, talking about the good times ahead. Little Lucie fell asleep in her father's lap.

Suddenly there was a loud knock on the door. Lucie gasped in fear. "Quick, Father— we must hide Charles at once!"

"No, Lucie, Charles is safe now. I'll go to the door and see who it is."

When Dr. Manette opened the door, four men pushed into the room. They wore red caps and carried weapons. Dr. Manette stared at them in shock. "What is this?"

"We have come to take Charles Darnay back to prison. He is under arrest."

"*Why?*" asked Dr. Manette. "What are the charges?"

One of the red-capped men took Charles by the arm. "I have no time to talk to you, old man," he said rudely to Dr. Manette. "Come to the trial tomorrow. Then you will hear about his crimes."

"Wait!" Charles said. "I have a right to know who has spoken out against me. Tell me who it is!"

The red-capped man gave Charles a hard, cold look. "Citizen Defarge and his wife, if you must know. Oh—and you are accused by one other person."

"Who?" Dr. Manette asked.

The red-capped man grinned. "Tomorrow you will learn his name, old man."

Without another word, they pushed Charles out the door. Dr. Manette tried to comfort Lucie as Charles was dragged off into the dark night.

9 Carton Makes a Plan

Mr. Lorry's head was bent over a pile of papers. Although it was very late, he was hard at work at the Paris office. He was startled to hear a loud pounding on his door. The caller was Sydney Carton. Mr. Lorry could hardly believe how different he looked. The man seemed to have pulled himself together. His face wore a very serious expression.

"I'm afraid I have some bad news," Carton said. "Darnay is back in prison. He was just arrested a short time ago."

"What?" Mr. Lorry exclaimed. "How can that be? Just a few hours ago he was set free. When I left him this evening, he was safe with his family."

"Believe me, it is true. I know a man who works in the prison. He told me that Darnay had been arrested for a second time."

"This fellow you know—can he help us?" asked Mr. Lorry.

Carton shook his head. "He doesn't have an important job at the prison. But he can get me in for one visit with Darnay."

"We must go at once to—" Dr. Lorry began, but Carton stopped him.

"There is no time! I have much to do before tomorrow. If the trial goes well, all will be well. But if it doesn't . . ." His voice trailed away. Carton did not want to say aloud what both of them were thinking.

After leaving Mr. Lorry, Carton walked to a nearby shop that sold drugs and medicines. When he told the chemist what he wanted, the man looked worried. "Well, sir, I can sell you those two drugs. But I must tell you how dangerous they are. Do you know what would happen if you mixed them together?"

"I do know," Carton said. "I promise to be very careful with them."

Carton paid for two packets of drugs and left the store. The hour was late. For a long

time he walked up one street and down another—as if he had no special place to go. Yet, Carton walked confidently—like a man who knows what he is doing. His head was high, his shoulders straight. It seemed that he had finally found something important to do with his life.

Hours later, the sun began to rise. Carton had stopped to rest on a little bridge over a river. As he watched dawn break, he thought about his father's funeral so many years ago.

"What was it the minister said on that

very sad day?" Carton asked himself. "They were the words that Christ spoke to his friends. Oh, yes—I remember now. *'I am the resurrection and the life. He who believes in me, even though he is dead, yet shall he live.'*" Carton smiled sadly.

The sun's first light shone across his face. Yet strangely, Carton's face seemed to be glowing from the inside as well as the outside. Again and again he softly repeated those long-remembered words.

The sun rose higher in the sky, lighting the city of Paris. Yet, for Charles Darnay and the other prisoners, the sun's rays brought neither light nor warmth to the dark, gloomy prison cells.

Once again, Darnay heard his name called to come to the courtroom. Once again he stood before five judges. As he looked out into the crowd, he saw Mr. Lorry, Dr. Manette, and Lucie.

"Charles Darnay, also known as St. Evremonde, you are an enemy of France. You are part of a cruel family, and all of you deserve to die," said the lawyer for the court.

Darnay turned pale. He could not believe what he was hearing.

"Who has accused the prisoner?" asked one of the judges.

"Citizen Defarge and his wife," said the lawyer. "And there is one other person—Dr. Alexandre Manette."

The people in the courtroom roared. *"Silence!"* the judge shouted.

Dr. Manette rose to his feet. His face had gone white. His body was shaking from head to foot. "That is an outrageous lie! How dare you say that I have accused my son-in-law!"

"Citizen Manette, be quiet now! Listen to the testimony," ordered the judge.

Dr. Manette sat down. Then, as Citizen Defarge came forward to tell his story, the room fell silent.

"Many years ago," Defarge began, "I worked as Dr. Manette's servant. After he was freed from prison, I took him to my home above the wine shop. There I cared for him until his daughter came from England. While he was in my home, I found that he did not remember his own name. He thought his name was the number of his cell—105, North Tower."

A low growl came from the crowd. Too many people remembered the horrors of being locked up in the Bastille.

"I visited Dr. Manette's old cell on the night the workers took control of the Bastille. When I searched it, I found some papers that Dr. Manette had hidden behind a stone in the wall. The papers turned out to be a diary the doctor had written while he was in prison."

"Do you have the diary with you?" the judge asked.

Defarge held up a pile of old papers. Then he continued, "Dr. Manette hoped that someone would find the diary so his story could be known. He wanted to show that he had done no wrong. He was sent to prison by an enemy—a nobleman who wanted revenge."

"Citizen Defarge," said the judge, "tell the court what is written in this diary."

Defarge then told the terrible story.

10 Dr. Manette's Diary

Dr. Manette's story begins one night in the year 1757. He was walking near the river when he heard a carriage speeding up behind him. Then suddenly, the driver pulled the horses to a stop. Dr. Manette turned to see what was going on.

A well-dressed man leaned out of the carriage. "You, there—are you Dr. Manette?" The doctor nodded. "Come along with me then. I must take you to someone who is in desperate need of a doctor."

Dr. Manette climbed into the carriage. He could see that this man was a nobleman. "Your name, sir?" Dr. Manette asked.

"I am the Marquis St. Evremonde."

"Who is my patient?" Dr. Manette asked.

"You'll find out soon enough," answered the Marquis. Dr. Manette saw that the man seemed annoyed rather than worried.

Before long the carriage pulled up to a grand mansion. The Marquis took Dr. Manette upstairs to a bedroom. There lay a beautiful young woman about 20 years old. She had a high fever. Tossing and turning, she called out for her father and then for her brother. It was clear to the doctor that the girl was very ill indeed.

"I can't do much for her," Dr. Manette said. "I will give her medicine to help her sleep—but she will not live much longer."

The Marquis shrugged as if he didn't much care. "There is another patient," he said. "Come with me."

The Marquis led Dr. Manette to the horse stables. In one of the stalls, a young man about 17 years old lay on a pile of straw. He had a deep knife wound in his side.

The doctor examined the young man, but he could see that it was too late. The boy was near death. "What happened to you?" asked the doctor in a gentle voice.

"My family rented farm land from the Marquis. He made us work hard, and he took everything from us—even our food! We had to pay high taxes, too. The Marquis stole my oldest sister to make her a servant. Our father died of a broken heart. I hid our younger sister so the Marquis could not steal her, too. Then I came to help my older sister, but he attacked me with his sword."

The young man glared at the Marquis. His eyes were filled with hate. "Someday, Marquis St. Evremonde, you will *pay* for what you have done! You and every member of your family will be punished!"

Shortly after that, the young man died. Then his sister died, too. Before sending the doctor home, the Marquis warned him not to tell anyone what had happened.

Dr. Manette did not promise to do as the Marquis asked. He knew the Marquis had a lot of power. But he also knew that what the Marquis had done was evil. At last, he decided to write to the police, telling how those deaths occurred. The doctor felt better when he took the letter to the police. He had done the right thing.

Then one night a carriage pulled up to

the doctor's house. A stranger dressed all in black came to the front door. He said that the police wanted to ask the doctor some questions about his letter.

The doctor went with the stranger. But he soon learned that this was a serious mistake. The stranger in black worked for the Marquis! He took the doctor directly to the Bastille—without a trial. Dr. Manette remained in a prison cell for 18 years. He called his cell a living grave.

At the end of his diary, the doctor wrote:

"I blame the Marquis St. Evremonde for what has happened to me. I curse the Marquis and every member of his family!"

When Defarge finished reading the diary, the crowd cried out for blood. "The prisoner Darnay is guilty! Take him to the guillotine! Cut off his head!"

"Charles Darnay St. Evremonde, you have been found guilty," the judge said in a stern voice. "You must die."

The red-capped guards started to lead Darnay back to his cell. Dr. Manette fell on his knees in front of Darnay. Tears flowed down the old doctor's cheeks. "Charles, please forgive me," the old man cried.

Darnay reached down and helped his father-in-law to his feet. "Dr. Manette, don't kneel to me, please. Now I understand why you were so upset when I told you my real name. But in spite of my cruel uncle's crimes, you tried to help me. I thank you with all my heart for your great kindness."

Lucie reached out to her husband for one last embrace. Both of them were sure they would never be together again.

At the back of the courtroom stood Sydney Carton. He had watched the whole trial with a heavy heart.

Escape to London

It was late that night when Sydney Carton walked through the door of Defarge's wine shop. Speaking very bad French, he ordered a glass of wine. He hoped Defarge and his wife would think he understood French as poorly as he spoke it. He was right! The Defarges did not lower their voices.

"Look at him," Defarge said as he poured the wine. "The Englishman looks very much like Darnay." Taking his wine with him, Carton sat down at a nearby table. He pulled a newspaper from inside his cloak and pretended to read. But he was listening closely to every word they said.

"St. Evremonde will die tomorrow," said Madame Defarge. She smiled and licked her lips. "But it is not enough. They must *all* die. The wife and child must die, too!"

Defarge frowned. "We have to stop the killing somewhere," he said. "Why should the wife die? Or even the child? What has the little girl done?"

Madame Defarge glared at her husband. "That farm family that was so cruelly treated by the Marquis was *my* family! The girl who died was my older sister! The boy who was stabbed was my brother! The father who died of a broken heart was my father!" She pounded the counter with her fist. "Those dead are *my* dead!"

Catching her breath, she went on. "You can try to tell the wind to stop blowing or the fire to stop burning." She pointed at the fireplace. "But do *not* tell me to stop hating! When I am done, there will be no member of that family left alive!"

Carton finished his wine and pushed his glass aside. He quickly left the shop and hurried to Mr. Lorry's office.

"Listen to me," Carton said when the door was closed. "Lucie is in great danger. The Defarges plan to have her put to death and—"

"*What?*" Mr. Lorry exclaimed. "But surely you don't mean—"

"Be quiet, I tell you!" Carton said. "Little Lucie is also in danger. They want her dead, too. There is no time to waste. You must help me get Dr. Manette, Lucie, and the child out of France! They must leave this terrible city for London tomorrow."

He reached into his wallet and pulled out a paper. "Here is my pass. Hold it for me. You must meet me tomorrow outside the prison gates. Have the carriage there at 2:00. Be sure that Lucie and her child and Dr. Manette are in the carriage. When I come, take me in quickly and drive away for London. Do not stop for anything or anyone."

"Very well," Mr. Lorry said uncertainly, as he took the pass. "But what—"

Carton firmly grasped Mr. Lorry's arm. "Promise me that you will do just as I ask." Mr. Lorry gazed into Carton's face. "I have a plan to free Darnay," Carton said softly. "But do not ask me anymore questions right now. Just make that promise."

Mr. Lorry nodded. "I promise," he said.

The next day, Carton went to the prison where his friend was waiting. "I need to be alone with Charles Darnay," he told the man. "I have a message for him from his wife."

Carton's friend nodded. "You will have to make it fast," he said, taking out a key and opening the cell door.

As Sydney Carton entered the cell, he saw Charles Darnay sitting at a table, writing some letters. He looked up in amazement. "Why, Carton—what are you doing here?" Darnay asked.

Carton put his finger to his lips. "Hush! We don't have time to talk. Quick—we must change clothes." As he spoke, Carton was already pulling off his boots. "Here, take these. Give me your boots!"

"This is crazy!" Darnay said. "There is no way to get out of this prison."

"I have a plan," Carton said. "You must *hurry*, Darnay! Do as I say."

Darnay leaned over to loosen one of his boots. Stepping behind him, Carton pulled a small bottle and a handkerchief from his pocket. He poured the liquid drugs onto the cloth. Then he grabbed Darnay and held the handkerchief over the man's nose.

Darnay tried to free himself, but in only a moment the drugs did their work. Out cold, Darnay fell to the floor.

Carton pulled off Darnay's shirt and coat and changed them for his own. He put his cloak around Darnay and pulled his hat down over Darnay's face.

At last he called the guard. When the cell door opened, Carton stepped back so that his face was deep in shadow. "Mr. Carton seems to have fainted when we were saying goodbye," Carton said. "Someone should carry him down to Mr. Lorry's carriage. He said it is waiting just outside the gate."

Everyone in the carriage was too upset to take a close look at the man they thought was Sydney Carton. When they reached the gates of Paris, the carriage was stopped by a guard. "Do you have your passes?" the guard asked.

Mr. Lorry handed the guard five passes. The guard read the names. He saw Lucie and her child and the old doctor. Then he looked at the man slumped in the corner. He seemed to be asleep.

The guard nodded. "Very well. Pass on."

As the gates of Paris closed behind them, Mr. Lorry took a long, deep breath.

Back in Paris, Madame Defarge was talking to a friend in the wine shop. "St. Evremonde dies today at the guillotine. Now it is time for his wife and child to die. I knitted their names into my list because they, too, are St. Evremondes."

Madame Defarge put her knitting aside. "I will go to their home now. No doubt they will both be crying for St. Evremonde. But he is an enemy of the French people—and crying for an enemy is also a crime!"

She hurried to the house where Lucie had been staying. When Miss Pross answered the door, she was surprised to see the sneering face of Madame Defarge.

"I demand to see the wife and child of St. Evremonde," Madame Defarge cried. "Let me in at once!" Pushing by Miss Pross, she wondered where to look first.

Miss Pross cleverly hurried to a closed

door and stood in front of it. She folded her arms across her chest. "You may not see her, you terrible woman," Miss Pross exclaimed.

Madame Defarge's eyes glittered with anger. "Get out of my way, you stupid fool!" she roared as she pulled a gun from her belt. Seizing Madame Defarge's arm, Miss Pross tried to make her drop the gun. Then all of a sudden, a shot was fired. Madame Defarge gasped, and then fell over. A bright red stain was spreading across her chest.

Miss Pross pushed the dead woman away. Her carriage for London was waiting just outside the door.

* * * *

Sydney Carton stood in one of the carts taking prisoners to the guillotine. There was no room to sit down. He was but one of *many* prisoners making the journey that day.

Carton did not look at the other prisoners. He seemed lost in thought. On each side of the street, crowds of people watched the carts roll by. Some laughed, some cried, some turned away in fear.

A young girl standing next to Carton began to cry. "I have done nothing wrong!" she sobbed. "I am just a seamstress—I make clothes. Why must I die?"

"Be brave, little one," Carton said. "Here, hold my hand. We will be brave together."

"You are so kind," said the girl. "What is your name, sir?"

"St. Evremonde," said Carton.

Searching his face, the girl frowned. "No, that's not true. You are not—"

"Hush!" Carton put his finger to his lips.

The girl looked at him and then shook her head. "*Why*? Why do you do this? Why would you die for someone else?"

"I do it for his wife and child," Carton said without hesitation.

The carts reached the guillotine. The great killing tool rose up like a hungry monster. It cast a black shadow over the prisoners. The smell of blood was in the air.

One by one the prisoners were led up the stairs. At the top, they were made to kneel down. Their heads were laid in such a way that the huge blade would cut quickly through the neck. *Whoosh!* Each time the blade fell, another head rolled into the basket.

It was time for the little seamstress to climb the stairs. Carton was alone. Gazing up at the guillotine, he thought, "I see a beautiful city. I see beautiful people rising up out of all this evil. I see the people for whom I am giving my life. They have good lives of peace and happiness. I see that they will never forget me—nor will their children nor their children's children."

Then it was Sydney Carton's turn to climb the stairs. Looking out across the city of Paris for the last time, he thought to himself, *"It is a far, far better thing I do, than I have ever done. It is a far, far better rest I go to, than I have ever known."*